For Emily

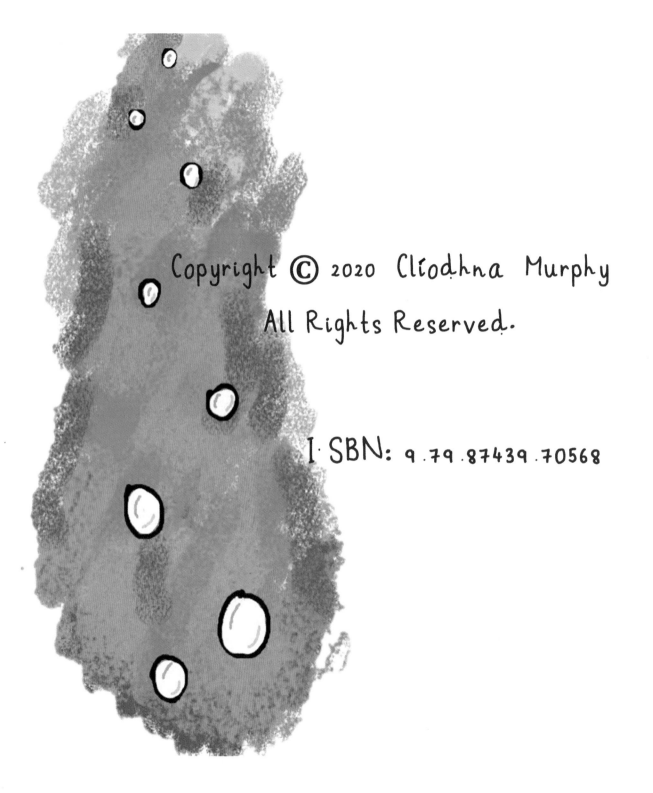

ISBN: 9.79.87439.70568

Berg

the Narwhal

Written and illustrated by
Clíodhna Murphy

This Berg book

belongs to

_____

This is Berg.

Berg is a Narwhal.

He has a large, strong body.

He has a tail like a dolphin,

fins like a whale

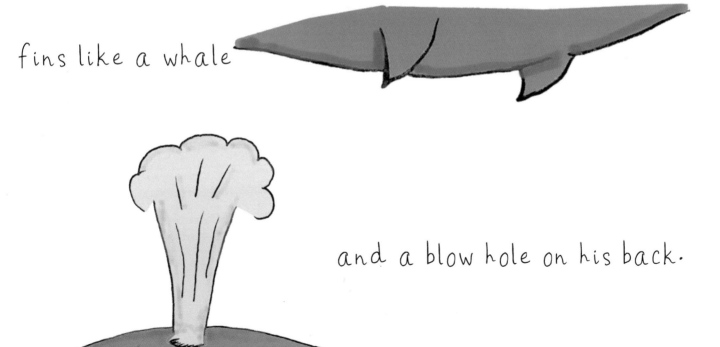

and a blow hole on his back.

But what is the best part about being a narwhal?

Berg has a long, pointy horn in the middle of his head. It makes him look like a unicorn!

Berg lives in Arctic city, a large underwater city where many different types of fish live together happily. Arctic city has...

tiny fish,

big fish,

round fish,

baby fish,

colourful fish,

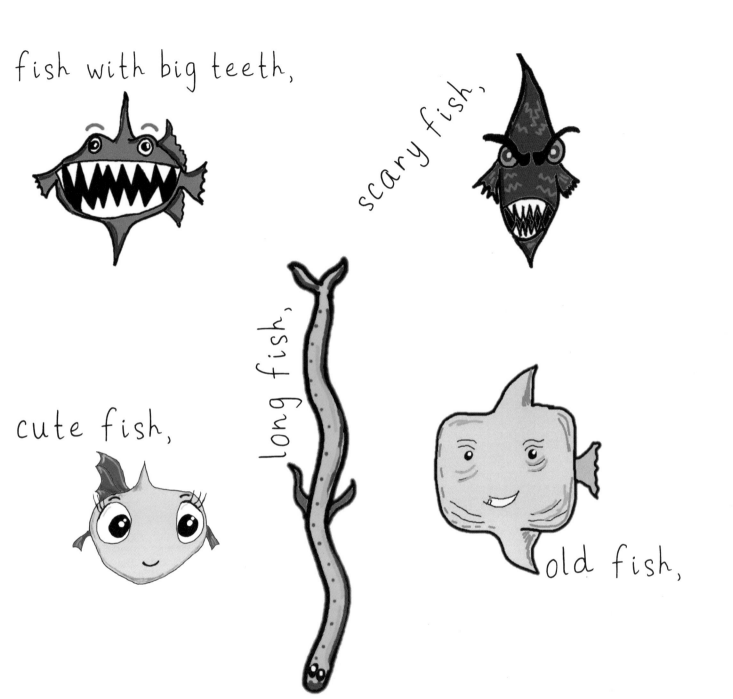

fish with big teeth,

scary fish,

long fish,

cute fish,

old fish,

and many many more...

Berg goes to Shell School. He is learning to be the best whale that he can be!

In his class, there are three more whales:

a humpback called Sam,

a blue whale called Nora,

and a killer whale called Finn

The other whales are not very nice to Berg. They treat him differently because he looks different to the others. No other whale has a tusk, like Berg.

They laugh at Berg,

they call him names,

and they leave him out of
their games.

One day, Sam, Nora and Finn were playing a game of Gulf Ball,

Berg was playing on his own.

The three whales wouldn't let Berg play, because they said his tusk would burst the ball.

All of a sudden, right in the middle of the game...

the Gulf ball was hit so hard, that it broke straight through the ice...

...and it bounced and bounced and bounced away from the hole in the ice.

What would they do?

The three whales argued and fought, blaming each other for loosing the ball.

How would they get their ball back from above the ice?

Soon, Sam, Nora and Finn stopped fighting and decided to come up with a plan to rescue their Gulf ball.

They picked all the things that they were good at and put them in their plan.

Each whale tried each plan....while Berg watched from the side.

Sadly, not one of the plans worked.

The Gulf ball was still stuck outside of the water!

As Berg watched, he had a great idea.

Berg smiled at the other whales and swam upwards as fast as he could.

Using his tusk, he made a hole in the ice, right under where the ball was.

Then he popped his tail through the hole that he made and pulled the Gulf ball back into the water.

The other whales who were watching Berg in amazement, all smiled and cheered!

Berg's Plan:
Step 1
Break ice with tusk.
Step 2:
Use tail to get ball back in the water.
Result: SUCCESS!

They all told Berg how amazing he was and how great it was that the tusk saved the day.

They were so impressed with Berg's plan.

Nora the blue whale, Finn the killer whale, Sam the humpback whale AND Berg the Narwhal played together happily with the newly rescued Gulf ball.

The best part about being a Narwhal is that I'm different to others. How boring would it be to be the same as everyone else?
I love my tusk and I am proud that I am the only whale to have one!

What makes you different?

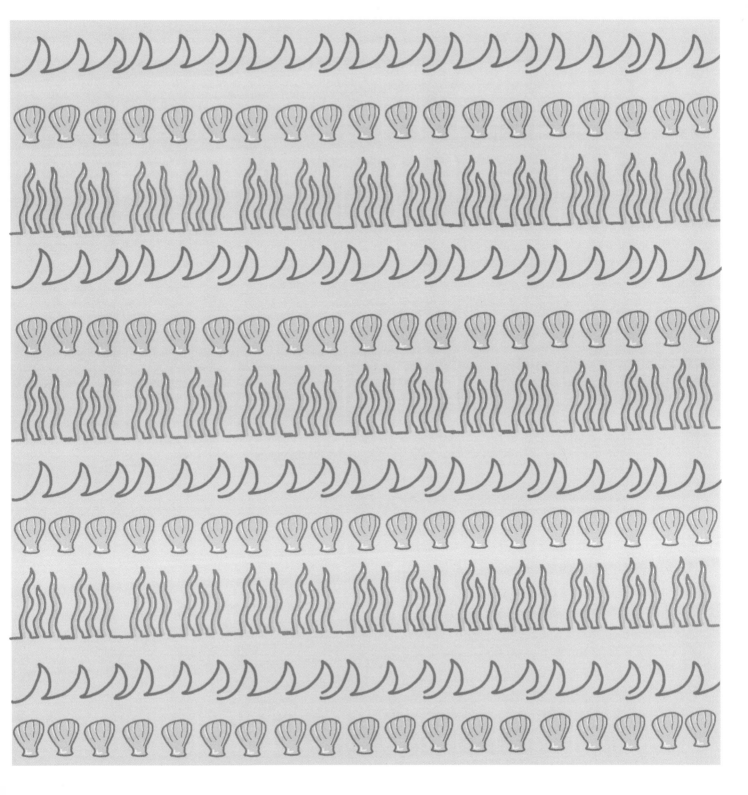

About the Author

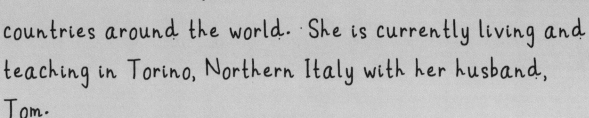

Clíodhna Murphy is a Primary Teacher from Kilkenny, Ireland who has travelled and taught in various countries around the world. She is currently living and teaching in Torino, Northern Italy with her husband, Tom.

Clíodhna has a passion for art and the Irish language and 'Berg the Narwhal' is her second children's picture book, after 'Fox Socks', which was released in 2020.

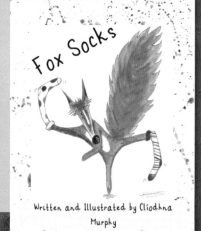

Printed in Great Britain
by Amazon

85779803R00020

Have you ever met a Narwhal?

Meet Berg!

Find out how Berg the Narwhal saves the day
and how he couldn't have done it without being
different from everyone else.

ISBN 9798743970568

90000

9798743970568